For my daughter Alice: Grow Alice, grow! G.F.

classic-minedition

English edition published 2020 by Michael Neugebauer Publishing Ltd., Hong Kong

Text and illustration copyright © 2007 by Giuliano Ferri
Original title: Wachse, kleine Kaulquappe
English text translation by Charise Myngheer
Rights arranged with "minedition" Rights and Licensing AG, Zurich, Switzerland.
Michael Neugebauer Publishing Ltd.,
Unit 28, 5/F, Metro Centre, Phase 2, No. 21 Lam Hing Street,
Kowloon Bay, Kowloon, Hong Kong. e-mail: info@minedition.com
This book was printed in November 2019 at L.Rex Printing Co Ltd
3/F., Blue Box Factory Building, 25 Hing Wo Street, Tin Wan, Aberdeen, Hong Kong, China
Typesetting in Big Caslo.
Color separation by Fotoreproduzioni Grafiche, Italy.
Library of Congress Cataloging-in-Publication Data available upon request.

ISBN 978-988-8341-92-4
10 9 8 7 6 5 4 3 2 1
First Impression

For more information please visit our website: www.minedition.com

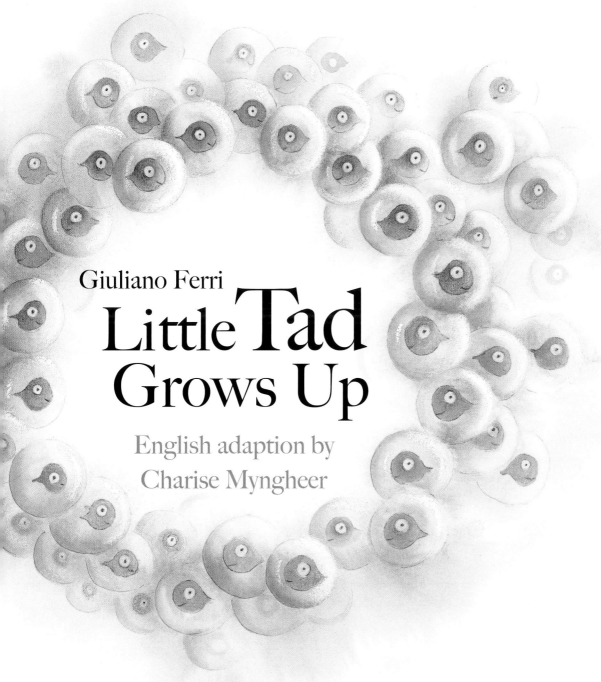

Giuliano Ferri

# Little Tad
# Grows Up

English adaption by
Charise Myngheer

classic-minedition

In the early Spring, Mother frog proudly laid her eggs
in the pond where she lived.
The small, dark eggs floated so closely together that they
looked like a big bunch of grapes. Each day, she checked
and waited for them to hatch.

For hours little Tad had been trying to think of a way to break out
of his soft shell. Unexpectedly, the egg began to twist and shake.
It shook faster and faster.
It shook so fast that suddenly it exploded, and Tad was free!

When Tad looked around, he realized
that he wasn't alone.
There were hundreds of tadpoles just like him.
They wiggled their tails in all directions.

"Wow! This is wonderful!" Little Tad said,
looking excitedly at his new world.

Tad's tail grew strong, and he learned to swim faster and faster.
Day after day, his mother proudly watched him from her lily pad.
Tad loved racing between the stems of the waterplants.
He was so fast that sometimes the wake he created sent the others
into somersaults.

The pond where Tad lived was beautiful. He had lots of friends,
and they played games together, like underwater baseball.

His tail was also very useful in getting him out of trouble or defending him against horrible bullies who you can always find – even in a pond.

Little Tad thought his life was perfect.
He never imagined that it could ever change...

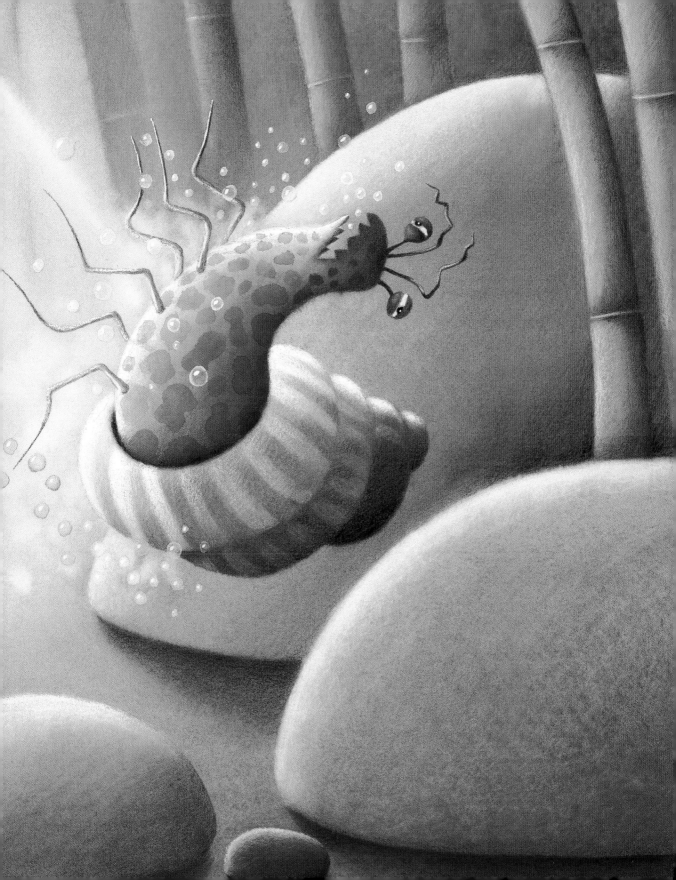

One morning, something terrible happened.
At first Tad thought he was dreaming. He had two strange things
poking out of his body. Tad shook his head to try to wake up,
but he was awake... and they were still there.
"Something's wrong with me!" he said in a panic.
"Mom! I'm turning into a monster!" Tad shouted.
"Those are just your legs," she said smiling.
"Someday you'll be glad you have them!"

Aunt Salamander overheard him.
"There's nothing wrong with you," she said. "You're just growing up."
"I don't want to grow up!" Tad said

Tad's two new legs felt strange. And before he even had time
to get used to them, two more appeared out of nowhere!
"Can things get any worse?" Tad asked himself.

Then he noticed that his tail was getting smaller!
"Grandpaaaa!" Tad said nervously.
"My tail is shrinking. I'm turning into a freak!"
But Grandpa just grinned.
"Losing your tail is completely normal, Tad," he said.
"You're just growing up."
"But I can't do anything without my tail!" Tad said.
"I don't want to grow up!"

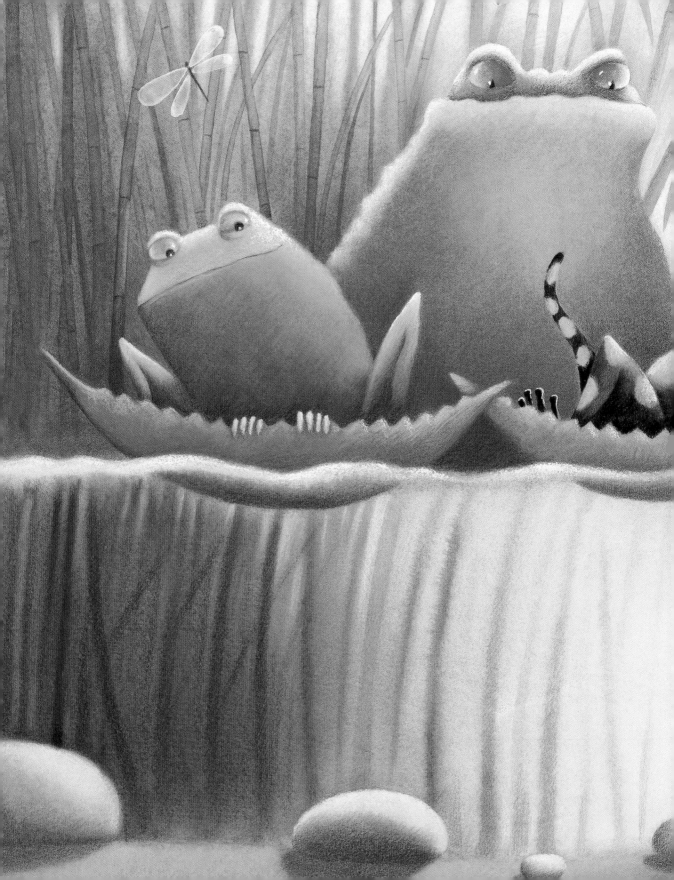

Everyone in the pond was trying
to reassure little Tad.
"You'll see, you won't need your
tail any longer when you are big,"
said Cousin Newt.
"You can do amazing things with
your legs," added the old prawn.

"Nobody seems to understand how I feel," Tad said sadly.
**"I REALLY DON'T WANT TO GROW UP!"**
And he began to cry.

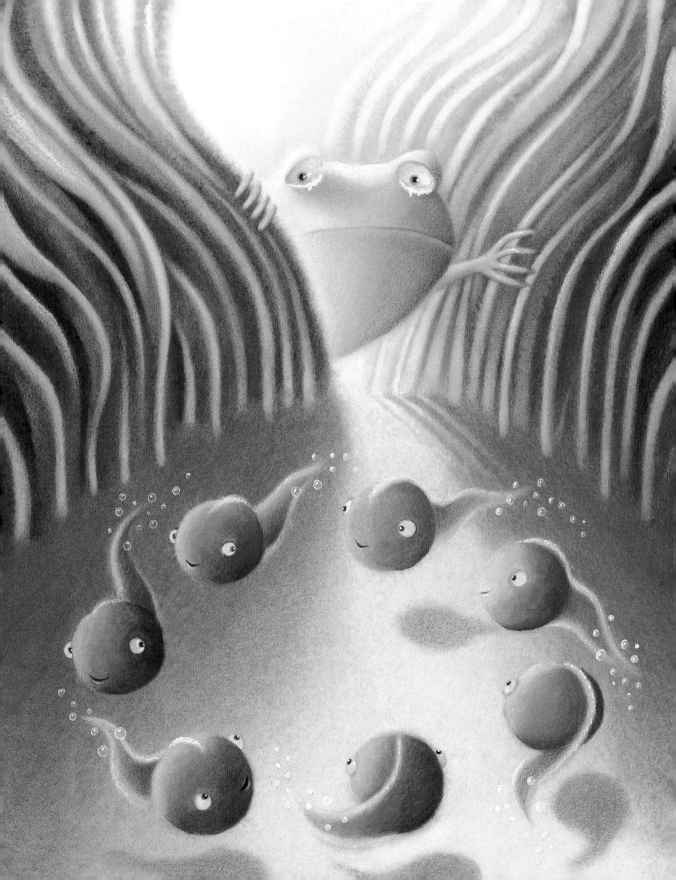

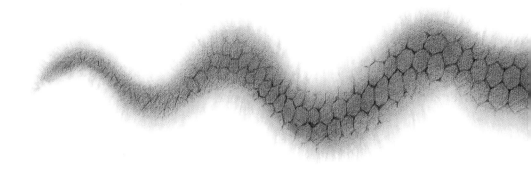

Tad wandered around the pond feeling sadder than sad.
Whenever he saw tadpoles playing, he felt jealous of their long,
beautiful tails. "You don't know how lucky you are," Tad said,
thinking about how things used to be when he was small like them.

Little Tad was so deeply absorbed in his thoughts that he did not
take any notice of the long, dark shadow above him.

It was a snake. "Normal... Sss-normal!"
hissed the sly snake. "They're wrong. Legs are useless. Look at me.
I don't have legs and I can move quicker than anyone I know."

"I want to have my tail back!" said Tad.
"I can't swim fast without it. Can you help me?"
"Of course," answered the snake. "But there's a secret to it.
Come a little closer to me."

Little Tad moved closer, and the snake opened his jaws wide.

As Tad stared deep into the snake's mouth, he was suddenly afraid.
His heart began beating faster, and his legs started to shake.
Suddenly, the snake hissed loudly and lunged toward Tad.
Tad's legs reacted naturally. With very little effort, he sprang high out
of the water and landed beside the pond!

Everyone cheered. "Wow!" Tad exclaimed.
"My legs are really strong!" As Tad looked around him,
he was amazed at all the new things he saw.
"Maybe growing up isn't so bad after all," Tad said,
jumping for joy.